OH, CHESTER !

WRITTEN BY
MICHELLE HINCK

ILLUSTRATED BY
BONNIE LEMAIRE

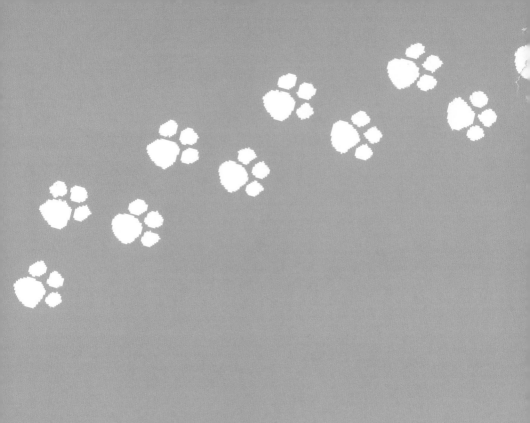

ISBN: 1492190306
ISBN 13: 9781492190301
Library of Congress Control Number: 1492190306
CreateSpace Independent Publishing Platform
North Charleston, South Carolina

Dedicated to the Holdens

Hi, everyone! It's me, Chester.

I know what you're thinking:

Wow, that is one handsome cat!

In case you didn't know, I am an elite breed, what they call a luxury cat. My fur is softer and silkier than any other, which is obvious the minute you meet me.

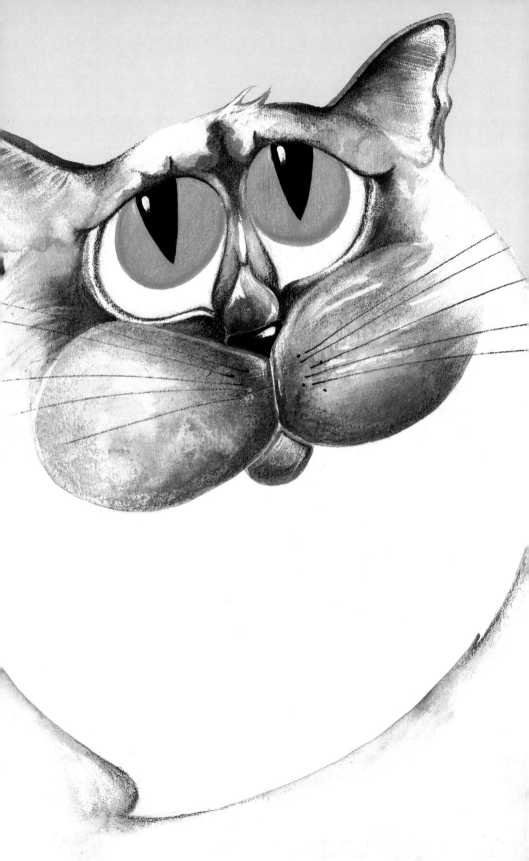

It's great being me, I must admit. I am strong. I am fast. I am extremely charming, and the girls can't seem to keep their hands off me. It's just one of those things that go along with being so good-looking, I guess.

I live like a king here in the Chester house.

My bowl is always full.

My litter box is always clean.

I even have my own water fountain to drink from.

When I am itchy, I simply roll over, and Mom scratches my belly.

When I am
bored, I say,
"I'm bored,"
and Brother
entertains
me.

When I am lonely, I say,
"I'm lonely," and Sister
snuggles me.

I spend most days
sleeping and sunbathing
on the patio.

In between naps, I must bathe to keep my fur in fine form. It's a full-time job being so good-looking, as you can imagine.

I have to snack throughout the day to keep up my strength, but don't worry. I have already informed everyone that I must not be disturbed during mealtimes.

Dad sometimes makes fun of how pampered I am around here, but it was his idea to bring me home, so clearly this is just jealousy on his part.

I have to admit at
this point, my friends,
that sometimes even
the cherished have
challenges. It's true.

One day, I was right in the middle of my early evening snack when Mom and Dad suddenly announced that they would be away for a few days. I didn't like the sound of this at all.

"I don't like the sound of this," I told them.

"Grandma is coming to stay with you," they said.

What? Who? I definitely did not like the sound of this.

"I object!" I said. I flattened my ears out so they would know that I was serious.

They left us anyway.
Days went by…

Sister hardly
snuggled me.

Brother was dreadfully
boring.

And the Grandma person
snored very loud.

"I object to this entire
situation!" I told everyone.

They ignored me.

When Mom and Dad came home, I really let them have it.

"Let me make it clear to you right now that I will not tolerate this irresponsible behavior in the future," I said.

They didn't hear me because they were preoccupied with the package they brought home. At least they had the decency to come home with a gift for me after all this...

Ugh!
What's that smell?

They opened the package and said, "There's someone we want you all to meet," and out came...a creature!

A screaming, screeching, bouncing, banging creature! The baby, they called it.

"What is the meaning of this?" I said.

They all ignored
me and fawned
over the creature.

"I demand an explanation!" I shouted. But it was like I didn't even exist. You can imagine the horror, I'm sure.

From then on, all they ever said was, "Oh, just look at the baby!"

"Oh, the baby is hungry."

"Oh, she's so cute!"
"Oh, look, she's growing some hair!"

"Oh, look at that; she pooped!"

No one ever cheers when I poop.

On and on it went.

"Look at her kick!"

"Look at her smile!"

"Oh, just look at her sweet dimple!"

You know what I say?

"Where's the love?"

"Oh, look at this picture of the baby!" they say.

You know what, friends? There are no pictures of me anymore without that stinky baby creature next to me.

I used to get brushed every day. Now my fabulous fur is full of knots.

I used to get held every day. Now Mom is too busy kissing the baby's fingers and toes.

I used to get food on demand. Now I have to wait until *she's* had *her* breakfast.

Where's the love, I say!

"Oh, Chester," they say. "Look at how she smiles at you. She loves you!"

Love? This is love? Plucking my whiskers and poking my eyes is love?

If having my fur pulled out by the roots is love, then I am going to need a lot of therapy.

Life is intolerable at the bottom, my friends. I don't recommend it at all.

"I never signed up for this!" I yelled when the baby looked at me.

"I strenuously object to the deplorable state of affairs around here!" I cried, and then I thumped my tail hard against the floor for effect.

Just then, something happened.

A strange noise came out of the baby creature. Was it a giggle?

Her eyeballs bounced up and down, following my thumping tail, and there it was again. Yes, it was a giggle.

This was an interesting development.

Giggle... Giggle ... ..giggle...

Thump, thump, thump, I whacked my tail hard on the floor. Giggle, giggle, giggle, she went.

Push, push, push, I pawed on her shoulder.

"Mmmm, mmmm, mmmm," she said, and relaxed.

Purr, purr, purr, I curled up against her.

And snore, snore, snore, that baby went right to sleep!

I should tell you right now that I have a patent on this technique. It works every time, and, therefore, I am back on top of the totem pole, people!

I put the baby to sleep, and my fur gets brushed.

I put the baby to sleep, and my bowl gets filled.

I put the baby to sleep, and then Mom has time to cuddle me again.

I win!

The End

Michelle Hinck graduated with degrees in theater and English from the University of Minnesota. She is the author of the bestselling, award-winning biography Great Love: The Mary Jo Copeland Story. Hinck currently lives in Wayzata, Minnesota, with her family, including Chester.

www.MichelleHinck.com

Made in the USA
Lexington, KY
02 November 2015